INVISIBLES

A Nature Friend publication
by Carlisle

Illustrated
by
Melinda Fabian

ISBN 1-890050-38-5

Carlisle

2727 TR 421
Sugarcreek, OH 44681

FISH FANFARE

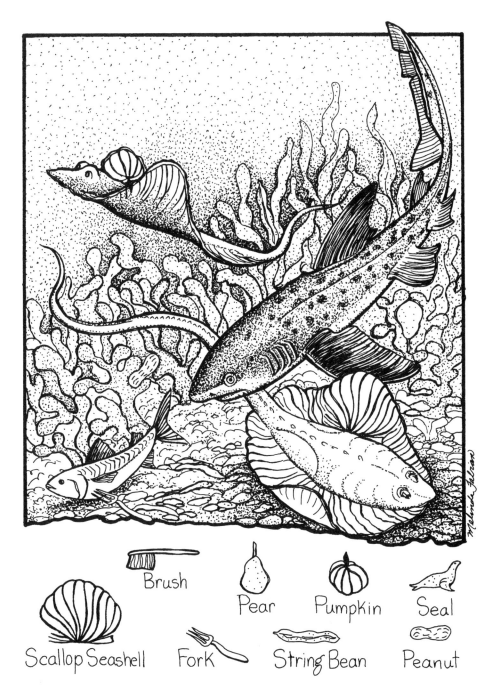

Brush

Pear

Pumpkin

Seal

Scallop Seashell

Fork

String Bean

Peanut

FOX & HARE

 Clam Shell

 Strawberry

Slice of Watermelon

 Turtle

Shoe

 Canoe

Pliers

 Duck

TOAD TREAT

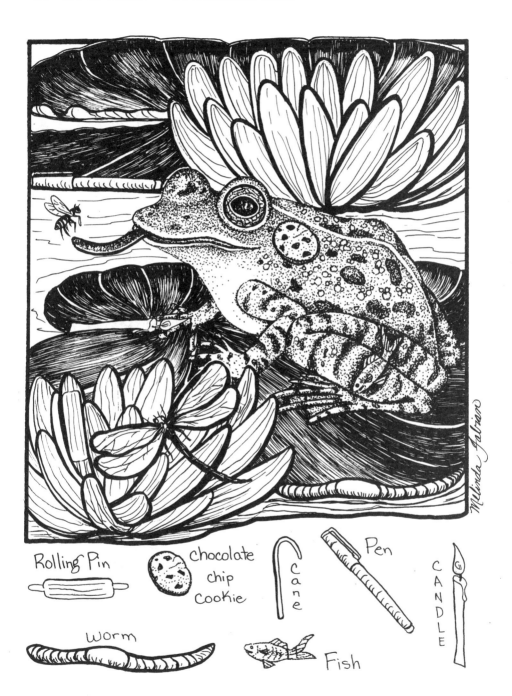

Rolling Pin

chocolate chip Cookie

Cane

Pen

CANDLE

Worm

Fish

OWL DINNER

Comb

Leaf

Seashell

Paper Clip

Spoon

Kite

Paint Brush

BUCK BATTLE

Screwdriver Leaf Tulip

Shovel Clothes Pin

Bowl Vase

BUTTERFLY TRIO

Straw-berry

Paint Brush

Safety Pin

Iguana

Bird

Spoon

Fish

WATCHFUL DOE

UMBRELLA

ICE
CREAM
CONE

RAKE

FISH

DUCK

BUTTER-
FLY

BRUSH

TEA
CUP

PHEASANT AFIELD

Melinda Fabian

Glove

Bird

Bumble Bee

Candle

Kernel
of
Corn

Nail

Turtle

Shoe

Paint Brush

FALL FOLIAGE

Pine Cone   Wheelbarrow   Scissors   Pig

Seashell   Paper Plane   Trowel   Kite   Tulip

HARVEST BLESSINGS

TEA CUP

SEASHELL

CLOTHES PIN

PEAR

STRING BEAN

MAPLE LEAF

PENCIL

CARROT

SWEET BOUQUET

Bird
Spoon
Paint Brush
Maple Leaf
Bat
Spatula
Starfish

SWALLOW FLIGHT

Mitten • Hammer • Leaf • Paint Brush

Spatula • Umbrella • String Bean • Clothes Pin

SNOW FUN

Bow
Pliers
Pumpkin
Mitten
Fish
Earthworm
Shoe
Comb

FRISKY FAWNS

Melinda Fabian

Acorn

Oak Leaf

Pine Cone

String Bean

Pencil

Ice Cream Cone

Eagle's Head

15

WINTER WINDOW

Tooth

Bird

Paper Airplane

Baby's Bib

Seashell

Fork

Rabbit's Face

WINGED WONDERS

Safety
Pin

Bat

Pear

Spoon

Seashell

Owl

Mushroom

Banana

ABOVE & BELOW

Pear
Rabbit's Face
Carrot
Strawberry
Shoe
Tree
Scissors
Acorn

HORSE & FOAL

Cat's Face Safety Pin Pear Turtle Banana Trowel Paint Brush Seashell

THE HUNT

FEATHER THUMB TACK PEAR MITTEN HAMMER OWL CUP BRUSH

COZY CARDINALS

Pencil

Pea Pod

Ice Cream Cone

Strawberry

Candle

Brush

Fish

Tomato

SUMMER BOUNTY

TREE SHOE MOUSE NAIL PENCIL BOOK ROSE

COATS OF ARMOR

Whale

Corn-on-the Cob

Seashell

Bird

Comb

Banana

Fork

HUNGRY BEAR

Spoon

Brush

Mitten

Pliers

Basket

Envelope

Cup

Shoe

MOUSE IN SPRING

COMB

PAINT-BRUSH

PENCIL

SPOON

STRAW-BERRY

SAIL-BOAT

CARROT

CROCODILE STYLE

Calendar

Comb

Paintbrush

Pear

Spatula

Scissors

Cook Pot

Snake

Melinda Fabian

BUNNY & BABIES

©Melinda Fabian 1997

PEAR

SPOON

SHOE

FEATHER

FISH

PAINTBRUSH

TULIP

Help Your Child
Discover THE Fascinating
World of Nature

- · 6" x 9"   · 36 pages
- · Full Color Photos and
  Art Throughout
- · ISSN 0888-4862

$22 1 year (12 issues) $40 2 years (12 issues save $4) $3 sample pak

$25 1 year Canada $30 1 year other foreign

N ature, from commonplace to phenomenal, delights children of all ages. *Nature Friend,* our monthly magazine for children, will educate your child about the world of nature. Its a world full of fascinating animals, birds, fish, trees, and flowers. Not to mention the sky, oceans, and the land. Your child will have hours of good, clean fun with the nature puzzles, nature stories, and science experiments. And it comes in monthly child size portions. Delight your children with these exciting monthly features: **Nature Mystery** (clues provided but you guess the animal) **Listen,**

You Can Draw

Children love to draw—
and to have their
drawings published!
This monthly drawing
project features a
selection of
budding artists'
submissions.

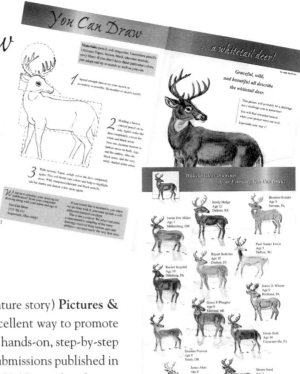

Look & Learn (a read-aloud nature story) **Pictures & Poems** (reader's submissions-excellent way to promote writing & art) **You Can Draw!** (hands-on, step-by-step art project—about 12 readers' submissions published in a subsequent month) **Who am I?** (Guess the identity of an animal) **Learning by Doing** (a hands-on science project for older children) **Lessons From Nature** (spiritual lesson drawn from nature). And then there are special feature stories—stories that make nature come alive in your child's mind.

And best of all, *Nature Friend* is in color! Color art and photographs are important to children! We keep that in mind as we work with our artists and photographers each month. If you want more reasons why your child will enjoy *Nature Friend*, write or call for a *Nature Friend* sample pak! ($3) Even better, enter a subscription today and bring the world of nature to your child's doorstep every month!

"*Nature Friend* magazine is a tremendous asset to any grade school cirruculum. This magazine produces brilliant pictures of nature. Look out *National Geographic*! There are stories, news, and experiments."

Kathy Banks in *Real Home School*

"Our children love *Nature Friend* magazine! It teaches nature facts in a lovely, uplifting manner that helps children learn about and enjoy the wonders of God's creation."

Mary Pride, homeschooling author and publisher

Carlisle
2727 TR 421
Sugarcreek, OH 44681

Subscribe Today!
Call 1-800-852-4482

Light on your Path

True Stories and Scriptures for Young Readers

- ILLUSTRATED!
- 6" x 9"
- 237 pages $**$10^{95}
- Paperback
- Color Laminated Cover
- ISBN 1-890050-35-0

PUT A SMILE ON THE FACE OF A CHILD—

Young readers love stories—real life stories. Stories about people. Stories about places. *Light on your Path* brings them page after page of stories that build a bridge between everyday situations and how God's Word teaches us to handle them . . . situations that require honesty, meekness, obedience, diligence, willingness . . .

You're always looking for ways to help with conflicts (serious and trivial) in your child's life. *Light on your Path* stories will reach young readers' hearts and minds for the Lord. He is the only One who is able and willing to take care of every detail of their young, impressionable lives!

Carlisle

2727 TR 421
Sugarcreek, OH 44681

Ages 7-14